CUMBRIA LIBRARIES

3 8003 05401 7934

KT-178-156

To Douglas fans everywhere.
THANK–YOU HUGS to you all for joining me
on this wonderful adventure.

One last thank you to Monika & Luka who
started this journey with me but have since . . .
well, grown into young adults!

www.davidmelling.co.uk

HODDER CHILDREN'S BOOKS

First published in hardback in Great Britain in 2021
by Hodder and Stoughton
First published in paperback in 2022

Text and illustrations copyright © David Melling, 2021

The right of David Melling to be identified
as the author and illustrator of this Work has been
asserted by him in accordance with the Copyright,
Designs and Patents Act 1988.

All rights reserved

A CIP catalogue record for this book
is available from the British Library.

HB ISBN: 978 1 444 90300 3
PB ISBN: 978 1 444 90301 0

1 3 5 7 9 10 8 6 4 2

Printed and bound in China

MIX
Paper from
responsible sources
FSC
www.fsc.org
FSC® C104740

Hodder Children's Books
An imprint of Hachette Children's Group
Part of Hodder and Stoughton
Carmelite House
50 Victoria Embankment
London, EC4Y 0DZ

An Hachette UK Company

www.hachette.co.uk
www.hachettechildrens.co.uk

HUGLESS DOUGLAS

GOES CAMPING

David Melling

Hodder
Children's
Books

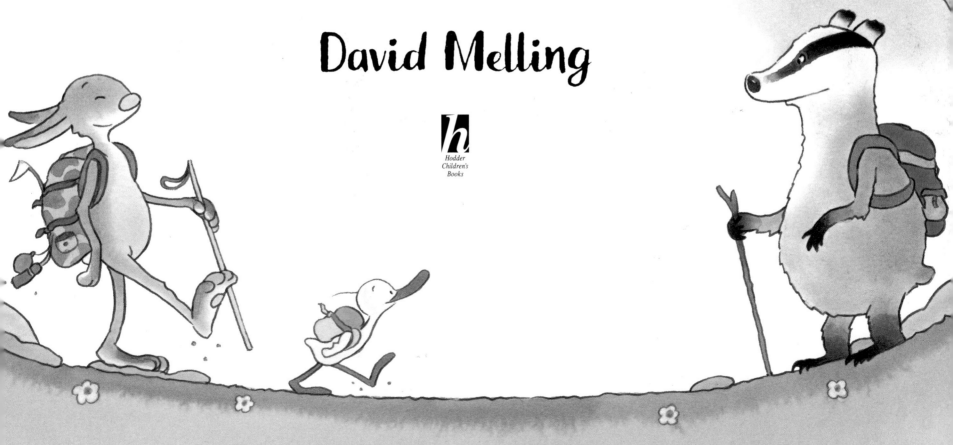

One evening, just as it was starting to get dark, Douglas packed up his big old tent and went to meet Badger, Rabbit, Little Sheep and Splosh.

They were all going CAMPING in Badger's Wood!

Douglas pulled out his tent, and together they tried
to make it into a tent shape.

Rabbit had brought her own tent.

'You should get one like mine,'
she said, 'it's automatic and pops
up in seconds!'

Eventually they got both tents up.
Douglas was so excited, he rushed inside and
changed into his pyjamas straightaway.

Everyone thought this was a great idea. And so did their **CUDDLIES!**

When they were all ready, they gathered
around Reading Rock with hot chocolate
and marshmallows.

'It's story time!' said Badger.
'Who has a good one?'

'Ooh, me!'
waved Little Sheep,
'I have a
spoooooky
story!'

'Once there were five friends who went camping
in the woods. But they soon got lost!
"It's getting dark," said one. "We'd better watch out for …

THE CUDDLY-SNATCHER!"'

'W-what's the Cuddly-Snatcher?' squeaked Douglas.

'The Cuddly-Snatcher goes, *"Ooooooo,"* in the night ...

He stomps about the woods with his rustly feet ...

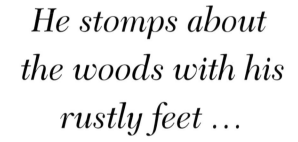

looking for cuddlies to snatch with his big grabby hands!

THE END!'

'Oh!' said Douglas.

'Don't worry,' chuckled Badger, 'it's only a story.
Time for bed!'

'Rabbit, do you want to
s-sleep in our tent?'
asked Douglas.

'I'm f-fine, thanks,'
said Rabbit with a
brave smile.

The others all squeezed
into Douglas' tent and snuggled
into their sleeping bags.

Suddenly, they heard a strange noise ...

'Ooooooooooooo!'

'What was *that?*'
whispered Douglas.

'It's probably Owl,' said Badger.
'Some creatures like being awake at night.'

'*I* don't like being awake at night,'
said Douglas.

'Neither do I!' called Rabbit
from her tent.

'I think I'd like to sleep in your tent after all,'
said Rabbit. 'Just in case.'

There wasn't much room,
but she managed to squeeze in ...

Everyone was just snuggling back down to go to sleep when they heard **rustly** footsteps outside ...

CRUNCH! CRUNCH!

then a **shadow** shivered across the tent ...

and suddenly a hand appeared!
Poor Douglas. It was too much ...

Rabbit, Splosh, Badger and Little Sheep all
tried to **catch up** with Douglas.

But he was too busy trying to run
in **four** different directions at once.

Eventually, Douglas ran out of puff.
The others gathered to calm him down.

'Douglas, it was
only me!' said Little
Sheep. 'When Rabbit
squeezed into our tent
I popped out!'

Back at Reading Rock, Badger made more hot chocolate.
'This time, let's try a nice *gentle* story,' he said.

Badger's story was magical and soon everyone felt much better – and *very* sleepy.

So the friends all snuggled up for a

HAPPY-CAMPING HUG

under the stars.

Goodnight!

CAMPING TIPS

Wrap up warm.

Torches are a camper's best friend!

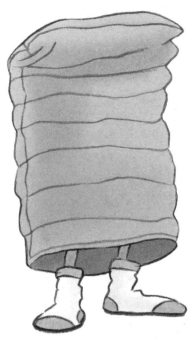

Don't forget a good story for bedtime (not too scary).

Make sure you know how to use a sleeping bag.

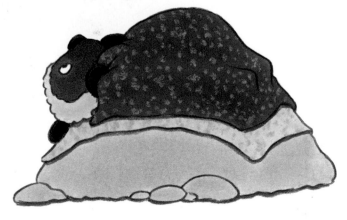

Choose a flat surface to sleep on – avoid lumpy rocks.

Check that your tent is big enough for everyone.

Buddy up in case of a
HUG EMERGENCY.

Read the
how-to-put-up-your-tent
instructions carefully.

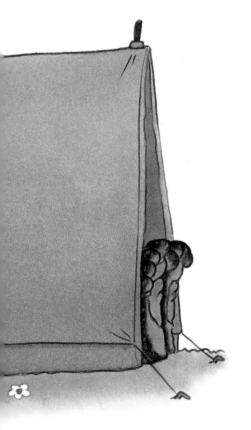

Bring plenty of hot chocolate
and marshmallows.

Don't forget –
plenty of cuddlies!

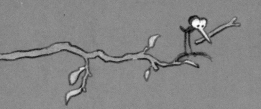

PICK-A-STICK!

What you'll need: a blindfold, sticks, a torch.
This game can be played outside or in a dark room.

One person sits blindfolded, holding the torch, with lots of sticks placed around them. The other players are split into two teams. The teams take it in turns to try and creep up and **pick a stick** and return safely to their starting position. If the stick-keeper hears a noise they shine the torch in that direction. If the torch beam lands on the stick-picker, they are out.

When all the sticks are gone, the team with the most sticks **WINS!**